GRANDMAS AT BAT

An I Can Read Book®

GRANDMAS AT BAT

By Emily Arnold McCully

HarperTrophy®
A Division of HarperCollins*Publishers*

To Sam Jones

HarperCollins®, 🎵®, Harper Trophy®, and I Can Read Book®
are trademarks of HarperCollins Publishers Inc.

Grandmas at Bat
Copyright © 1993 by Emily Arnold McCully
Library of Congress Cataloging-in-Publication Data
McCully, Emily Arnold.
  Grandmas at bat / by Emily Arnold McCully
    p. cm. — (An I Can Read book)
  Summary: Pip's two grandmothers, who cannot agree on anything, take
over coaching her baseball team and create chaos.
  ISBN 0-06-021031-1. — ISBN 0-06-021032-X (lib. bdg.)
  ISBN 0-06-444193-8 (pbk.)
  [1. Baseball—Fiction. 2. Grandmothers—Fiction.] I. Title. II. Series.
PZ7.M478415Gs   1993   92-8318
[E]—dc20   CIP
                                                                   AC

First Harper Trophy edition, 1995.

Contents

No Coach

"Our coach has chicken pox!"

said Pip,

"and our first game is on Saturday!"

"What a shame," said Mom.

"They will not let us play

if we cannot find a new coach,"

said Pip.

"I love baseball,"

said Grandma Sal.

"I could be your coach."

"Oh, Sal," said Grandma Nan,

"you don't know what a coach does."

"Yes I do," said Grandma Sal.

"I watch the games on TV."

"Watching is not doing,"

said Grandma Nan.

"I have played baseball.

I will help."

"I didn't know you played baseball,"

said Grandma Sal.

"You don't know lots of things,"

said Grandma Nan.

The telephone rang.

It was Ski.

"Bad news," he said.

"We can't find a coach.

The game will be called off."

"Maybe it won't," said Pip.

"I have two coaches right here."

"Who?" asked Ski.

"Grandma Nan and Grandma Sal,"

said Pip.

"Your *grandmas*?" cried Ski.

"Pip, we have a big game

on Saturday!"

"So we will practice," said Pip,

"and the grandmas can watch."

"But you know your grandmas . . ."

said Ski.

"As long as we can play," said Pip,

"who cares who is coach?"

Practice

"Yoo-hoo, Stings,"

called Grandma Sal.

"How do you do, team,"

said Grandma Nan.

"This is Dolores, Julio, Aggie,

14

Mona, Tad, Grace, Norman,

and you know Ski," said Pip.

"What a big team!" said Grandma Sal.

"It's nine players, Sal,"

said Grandma Nan.

"That is a baseball team!"

"Time for warm-up exercises!"

said Grandma Nan.

"Come on, Sal, show the team!"

"You first, Nan," said Grandma Sal.

"Show them how you do push-ups."

"Grandmas," said Pip,

"we know what to do.

We need to practice playing."

"Okay," said Grandma Sal.

"Hold up that glove, Nan.

Watch how I throw," said Grandma Sal.

"Oops!"

"Sal, they should practice batting.

You are up first," said Grandma Nan.

"Nan, you are a bossy boots!"

said Grandma Sal.

"I am the coach!" said Grandma Nan.

"Coaches give orders."

"Not to other coaches,"

said Grandma Sal.

"Do something, Pip," said Ski.

"Your grandmas are

driving us bananas!"

"Grandmas, stop!" cried Pip.

"Okay," said Grandma Nan.

"I will hit first."

21

"Sal, I can't hit your pitches,"

said Grandma Nan.

"It takes a while to warm up,"

said Grandma Sal.

CRAAACK!

"Wow," said Grandma Sal. "Run, Nan!"

"The coaches are hogging the field!"

cried Grace.

"Grandmas!" Pip yelled.

"*We* need to practice playing!

Please sit on the bench and watch!"

"Just watch?" said Grandma Sal.

"Not coach?" said Grandma Nan.

"We all *know* what to do!" said Pip.

"You do?" asked Grandma Sal.

"Of course!" said Pip.

"All right," said Grandma Nan.

"Go and play," said Grandma Sal.

"Hooray!" cried the Stings.

The grandmas watched.

"These kids are good,"

said Grandma Sal.

"They don't need us,"

said Grandma Nan.

28

"I feel left out," said Grandma Sal.

"I do too," said Grandma Nan.

"You know, Nan," said Grandma Sal,

"I think I know a way we can help!"

"Oh, Sal," said Grandma Nan,

"I think I know too!"

The Game

It was Saturday.

The Stings were waiting

to play the Grubs.

"Where are the grandmas?"

asked Ski.

"I don't know," said Pip,

"but I know they will come."

"I hope they don't do

anything funny," said Aggie.

"They won't," Pip said,

and crossed her fingers.

"Yoo-hoo!"

"Grandmas!" cried Pip.

"Uh-oh," said Mona.

"They look weird!"

"You can just watch us play, okay?"

said Pip.

"Don't worry about us, Pip,"

said Grandma Nan.

"Batter up!" called the umpire.

The Grubs were first at bat.

Pip pitched.

Three Grubs got base hits.

Ski went to the mound

to talk to Pip.

"What is the matter?" he asked.

"It's my grandmas," Pip said.

"They look so silly."

"Just think about pitching,"

said Ski.

But the next Grub hit a double,

and another Grub hit a home run.

Then a Grub hit a pop fly,

and Aggie caught the ball.

37

Ski made a double play.

The score was now Grubs 5, Stings 0.

It was the Stings' turn to bat.

Dolores hit a long drive,

but it was caught.

Aggie hit a fly to third base.

Pip struck out.

In the sixth inning

the score was Grubs 6, Stings 0.

"This is hopeless," said Julio.

"We cannot get a hit."

"Nan, this is not good,"

said Grandma Sal.

"The team needs us now!"

said Grandma Nan.

"That's right!" said Grandma Sal.

"Let's go!"

Grandmas Go to Bat

It was the last inning.

The grandmas jumped off the bench.

"Rah team rah!" they cheered.

"Sis boom bah!"

"Oh no," said Pip.

"Not now, Grandmas," said Ski.

"The ball has wings

when it's hit by Stings!"

the grandmas shouted.

"Put the Stings to the test;

they are the best!"

46

"They think we're the best,"

said Dolores.

"On the mound,

on the bases,

in the field,

Stings are aces!"

cried the grandmas.

They shook their pom-poms.

"Maybe we *can* win,"

said Norman.

"Shake them up,

shake them up!"

the grandmas yelled.

"You can do it, Stings,"

called the crowd.

"Huzza huzza,

pow pow pow!

Sting them, sting them,

now now now!"

shouted the grandmas.

"Hear that, team?" said Pip.

"Let's win it for the grandmas!"

"All right!" yelled the Stings.

"Strike them out!"

yelled Grandma Sal.

"You can do it!"

Pip struck out three Grubs.

When the Stings went to bat,

Mona hit a single.

"More hits," cried the grandmas.

Ski hit a double.

Tad hit a home run.

"We're not quitters;

we're home-run hitters!"

the grandmas shouted.

Grace hit another home run.

Then Julio hit a triple,

Dolores hit a double,

and Mona hit a home run.

The score was Stings 7, Grubs 6.

The Stings had won!

"We won it for the grandmas,"

said Ski.

"You won it because

you are the Stings,"

said Grandma Sal,

"and the Stings are the best."

"Thanks, Grandmas," said Pip.

"You are welcome,"

said Grandma Nan.

"Well, Sal, I will never forget today.

It was fun being a cheerleader."

"Grandmas," said Pip,

"we want you to cheer

at every game we play."

"Oh my," said Grandma Sal.

62

"What do you think, Nan?"

"I think we need new pom-poms,"

said Grandma Nan.

"These are worn out!"

Then the Stings yelled,

"On the field

and at the plate,

who makes sure

the Stings are great?

Grandmas, Grandmas,

Grandmas, YAY!"

64